Don't Forget to Smile

Dedicated to my mother

**She taught me how to tackle the difficult days
and find reasons to smile**

We all have bad days.

Days when we don't want to show our face.

And we want to hide away.

When you feel down, think of things that bring you joy.

Like a warm blanket.

And sunny days.

Rainy days too!

Do something that makes you happy.

Like taking a nap.

Or hanging out with a friend.

Go outside and be active.

Stay in bed and rest.

Tell a joke.

Give a friend a hug.

And most importantly, don't forget to...

Smile!

And keep smiling!

And smile some more!

The end.

Printed in Great Britain
by Amazon

12880770R00025